THE WOMBANDITOS

A Prequel Humorous Fantasy Novella

THE WESTERN LANDS AND ALL THAT
REALLY MATTERS

ANDREW EINSPRUCH

Cover design by Maria Spada of Maria Spada Design.

Editing by Vanessa of Red Dot Scribble.

Proofreading by Abigail of Bothersome Words.

Layout by Andrew Einspruch of Wild Pure Heart.

ISBN: 978-0-9806272-4-4

To Billie and Tamsin

Everything of greatest value that I've learned, I've learned from you.

🏵 I 🏵

HOCKEY SACKING

Eloise Hydra Gumball III, Future Ruler and Heir to the Western Lands and All That Really Matters, raced across the Culpability Courtyard, trying not to get slammed by a pack of people twice her size. Centuries before, criminals, miscreants, traitors and minor offenders had been dragged into the courtyard and flogged, pilloried, beaten or soundly chided. Now, the castle's internal field was devoted to the third most popular pastime in all the realms: hockey sacking.

The hockey sack in the 16-year-old princess's left arm was light enough to carry easily, but heavy enough to feel substantial and to slow her down a little as she sprinted toward the far end of the field. Eloise had snatched the hockey sack from the Them team's grunter as he bounced it on his knees and elbows. She'd snuck up behind him and snagged it with a diving catch, then rolled out of the dive, scrambled back to her feet, and headed off. As changer, it was her job to get the hockey sack to the other end without getting creamed by a defensive girder or having it stripped from her by the left or right flutter. There, she'd either try to knee-knee-kick it through the basket-shaped goal, or knee-knee-knee-ankle tap it to the middle splendid, who'd belly-trap it then elbow-elbow-elbow-elbow it past the other team's retainer and into the brass vase beside the goal.

Eloise had a changer's shape—willowy and lithe—and her handmaid, Odmilla de Platypus, had tied her unruly, dark curls into a changer's braid, which thumped her in the back as she pounded down the field. Eloise dodged one defensive girder, slipped past a second, then spun to get away from a third. As she got close to the basket, she decided to be fancy: knee-knee-foot-foot-head (left)-head (right)-dropkick. The kick was supposed to swish into the back of the goal, bounce out, then rim back in for two points instead of one. She would have sunk it, too, except the extra moves gave the other team's left defensive girder time to blindside her. The girder, a woman with the build of a decent-sized shed, flattened Eloise into the turf, grabbed the hockey sack out of the air, avoiding a down, and ankle-ankle-ankle-ankled it to her own changer, who rushed away.

Eloise spat out several blades of grass and accepted the woman's hand to help her up. In other circumstances, the princess would have waved it off with a polite smile, allowing her habits their sway (it was easier than wondering what agues might lurk in their systems). But here on the Culpability Courtyard, she always swallowed back those inclinations in favor of the camaraderie of the game. Hockey sacking was the one great equalizer at Court. Everyone played hard and played their best, be they royal, noble, or naught.

Jerome Abernatheen de Chipmunk, Eloise's friend for a decade, was too small to play, so he kept score. When Eloise went down, he raised a purple flag with his tail, rang the gong once, and called out, "Point to Them for stripping the hockey sack."

The defensive girder punched the air, triumphant. "Go, Them!"

Eloise whirled and looked at Jerome. "Really, Jer? You gave her a point? For that? Were you even watching?"

"Easy there, Princess Eloise. No arguing with the scorekeeper."

"I wouldn't argue if the scorekeeper did his job properly, instead of wafting off with his cup of haggleberry tea."

Jerome set down his cup and saucer. "The changer for Us should focus on where she's carrying the hockey sack, as well as the relative positions of the Them players, instead of taking issue with the impartial, attentive and exceptionally fair scorekeeper, who carefully balances his calls of 'Go, Us!' and 'Go, Them!', thereby demonstrating said impartiality."

Eloise snorted in mock outrage. "The scorekeeper's attention extends to his tea and, if he stretches, to his plate of Chef's almond butter chews."

Jerome wiped almond butter chew crumbs from his whiskers and gave the princess an exaggerated I-don't-really-want-to-do-this-but-you-made-me look. He raised the purple flag with his tail and rang the gong again, saying, "Point to Them. Sassing the scorekeeper and mocking his almond butter chews."

Eloise blew a raspberry at him and he returned the gesture, adding a sarcastic tail shake and whisker wobble. She turned back to the game just in time to catch the hockey sack as the Us left flutter lateraled it back to her. She sped away toward the goal, hotly pursued by both Them defensive girders.

2

HOP A CART

After the game, which—to Eloise's embarrassment—had ended in Them winning by a single point, both teams and the small crowd moved to a sunny area for a post-game convivium. The long tradition of food and beverages after the final flag helped ensure that any on-field rivalry melted back to friendliness, thereby keeping peace at Court. Servants (a couple of whom had just been playing) served bubbling cider, haggleberry tea and haggleberry chai, bowls of fruits that were surprising to see this late in autumn, a savory jackfruit curry, and abundant platters of Jerome's almond butter chews.

Eloise and Jerome sat on a bench with a lovely view of a sycamore, whose leaves wafted down in the occasional breeze. "I didn't deserve that penalty point," the princess said. Taking a knife and fork, she sliced a rectangular almond butter chew into exact quarters, then eighths, arranging the pieces into pairs by combining one and eight, two and seven, three and six, and four and five. She would eat them in that order when she was ready. Her rituals were her rituals, and her habits were her habits. She simply preferred doing things just so—it made her feel better, or at least right, for a while.

"Of course you deserved it. You're lucky I approach scorekeeping with benevolence and tolerance. It might have been two points." Jerome sipped his tea (never sweetened) and sighed. "Chef really can brew a perfect tea, when she has a mind to. I can tell from the taste when she's feeling relaxed and happy, and when she's hassled and passed the tea preparation to one of her scullery hands."

The pair sat in silence, enjoying the food, the breeze and the spectacle of the leaves. "I've missed this," said Eloise. "Spending time together." She rubbed her calf, feeling a sore spot. There would be a deep purple bruise by nightfall, a souvenir of the game.

"Court makes it harder, for sure. You're busy all the time. It's not like it used to be, when our biggest concern was distracting Chef enough for one of us to snatch a couple of brioches, or worrying about memorizing one of the Venerable Prelate Herself's interminable devotional lists about Çalaht. I mean, the lists in the *Scrolls of Çalaht* are bad enough on their own. But the Venerable Prelate Herself's tutelage also had all of those lists she created, supposedly to help with learning."

"I know," said Eloise. "The 18 Miraculous Visions Involving Cutlery."

"The 23 Supplications to Use on Snowy Days."

"As if anyone would care, or even use them." Jerome sipped again, then nibbled a slice of peach, which must have found its way from The South. "How about the 52 Tedious Passages That Really Are Important?"

"That one I have to give her," said Eloise. "They were definitely tedious. Incredibly so. But if you want to understand the foundational teachings from the Divine One, they do help."

"I wouldn't know," said Jerome. "I couldn't bring myself to read them."

A few more minutes passed as they ate in comfortable silence.

"You know what would be fun?" said Eloise.

"What?"

"Going somewhere. Just sneaking off for a day. Away from the demands of Court."

"Good luck with that. The queen has you booked solid."

"Tell me about it. If it isn't a reception for an olive enthusiasts club visiting from the Eastern Lands, it's a reception for a wart cream merchants association from the Half Kingdom. She says it's good for me to attend these things, that it will help me get used to hobnobbing and kibitzing, and start making connections with people from the four-and-a-half realms."

"Wart cream connections could be important someday."

"Crucial to peace in our times, I'm sure." Eloise took another almond butter chew and placed it in the exact centre of the folded serviette on her tray, but did not cut it up yet. "I love the colors this time of year."

"When I was a pup, my mother used to take me to Waft! An Autumnal Festival."

"What's that?"

"A local festival at Mooondale that celebrates autumn. It's named after the leaves that waft down from above."

"Never been. That's, what, half a day's cart journey from here?"

"Less. Much less, depending on how you travel. Mooondale has huge stands of deciduous trees, like gingko, smokebush and maple. At this time of year, people come from all over to see the colors and drink the famous secret punch that's made from a carefully guarded blend of yellow, orange and red ingredients."

"Sounds fun. I wish could go."

"So go."

"Can't. Too much going on. Really can't." Eloise put her plate down on the tray. "But nice thought, anyway."

"Come on, El. Let's go together. You really think the wart cream enthusiasts will miss you?"

"It was olive enthusiasts, and no, they probably wouldn't. It's not like they're here to see me."

"So, play hooky. Feign an ague. We could catch a ride with a merchant going down the Queen's Road, get to Mooondale, see some trees, have some punch, hop a cart coming back toward Brague, and have you at the dinner table in time to say, 'I'm feeling better now, thanks.' Easy."

"Tempting."

Jerome jumped up, excited. "You should see the trees, Ellotastic. Yellows and golds and oranges and auburns and reds and every shade in between." He pointed at the sycamore. "It's like this, times a hundred. Times a thousand."

"Would it work?"

"Of course it would work, El. Come on. Live a little."

"Whizzing off in secret for a day is really not the sort of thing I do, Jerissimo."

"All the more reason to do it. Soon, Court is going to suck up every second of your life. Even more than it does now. You think it will be easier to sneak away then?"

"No."

"So, let's sneak away now."

"Mother will kill me."

"Only if the queen finds out. Which she won't."

Eloise poured another cup of haggleberry tea and placed it and the pot equidistant from the edges of the tray. She checked in with her habits about the excursion. None of them were screaming, probably because the travel would be brief and by cart. And Jerome was right. The pile of obligations and commitments would only grow. Waft! An Autumnal Festival sounded lovely, and not that far away. Would anyone really miss her? Not her twin sister, Johanna. They weren't talking that much anymore. Odmilla might, but Eloise could make sure she disappeared after breakfast, when Odmilla was busy handling laundry. She could send a messenger herald to let her mother know she wasn't feeling well and would have to miss whatever it was that was going on.

"How would we find a cart?"

"Radishes."

"Radishes?"

"Radishes. The radish mongers from Lower Glenth go past Mooondale to get here. We just have to find one of them heading home. I can find one. What do you say?"

"I say this is a bad idea."

"El, do you remember passage 36 from the Venerable Prelate Herself's list? The one where Çalaht praises the leaves of a liquidambar, and talks about the impermanence of all that one grasps onto as precious?"

"I thought you didn't read them."

"I read that one. The liquidambar thing happens right before that whole horrible episode with her thumbs. But it's dull, like the Venerable Prelate Herself says, so people skip it."

"Are you suggesting that slinking out of the castle for a day of foliage observation would be an important step in one's spiritual understanding of the life of Çalaht?"

"Nope, but that sounds like a good argument."

Eloise picked up a sycamore leaf and twirled it in her fingers. "See what the radish monger situation is. I'll see what's on the agenda for tomorrow. I might be feeling a bit peaked after all."

"That's the spirit!" Jerome bowed formally and went down on one knee. "It would be my honor to abscond with the princess to enjoy a few hours of autumnal gazing at Waft! An Autumnal Festival."

"Thank you, Master Jerome."

"Now, are you going to eat that last almond butter chew, or what?"

❦ 3 ❧
IN A CIRCLE

That night, Odmilla brushed out Eloise's curled mess of hair, a ritual Eloise enjoyed. Before the platypus became her hand-maid, having a nanny or servant do her hair was a penance at best, and a torture at worst. But Odmilla's clever, patient paws could coax out even the most determined knots, a knack Eloise swore bordered on weak magic. She learned to relax as Odmilla methodically separated her hair into strands and tugged it gently with wide-toothed combs, and sometimes, if the styling was ambitious enough, narrower combs.

"Princess, what sort of braid do you fancy this evening?" asked Odmilla. Her rubbery platypus snout and her heavy, rural Southie drawl made it difficult to understand, but Eloise was used to it by now.

"Whatever suits, I guess. Something simple and tight. We'll save frilly, complicated, and message-laden for another time, don't you think?"

"As you wish, Princess. Do you have a preference for ribbon color?"

Eloise thought about the outfit she planned to wear the next day. "Navy blue, please."

"Oh, a change. Well, you know what they say. A change is as good as having your blood replaced."

"Not a great phrase, really."

"No, Princess. Not really."

Her hair done and dressed for bed, Eloise bid her handmaid goodnight and blew out the candle. She then drank a full volume of water to make sure she woke up early.

❦

IN THE PRE-DAWN LIGHT, ELOISE DRESSED HERSELF IN SENSIBLE clothes suitable for travel at that time of year, left Odmilla a note that would not cause alarm, slipped out of the family living quarters, and went to the rendezvous point Jerome had specified: the Dangling Participle, a public inn favored by poets, bards, and sticklers about language.

The cart that Eloise and Jerome rode on belonged to a stout radish monger named Bööster Böyden, who everyone called BB. His "going to town" crofter's clothes looked well-mended and clean (Eloise suspected a loving spouse), his complexion reminded Eloise of a turnip, and his hair shared the exact texture, form and shade of brown as a particular flocked rug in one of the castle's guest rooms. They sat on the back of the cart, feet dangling off, leaning against the crates. Jerome had even organized a cushion and blankets to keep them warm and keep dust off Eloise, which would help keep her habits in hand.

The cart was pulled by a chipper, chatty bay horse named Basilio de Bardigiano, who went by BdB. Jerome had found them waiting for their radish crates to be filled with pears for their return trip to Lower Glenth. BB and BdB were equal partners in a transport enterprise. Their cart sported a jaunty, hand-painted cartoon of a giant radish with cart wheels featuring cartoon likenesses of BdB and BB. Below this were the words "Radish Rollers: Transporters of Fine Radishes and Radish-Related Products." Then, in smaller letters: "You have Radishes. We have wheels. Let's roll!!!!" They'd been happy to accept a few of Jerome's coins in return for a spot on the back of their cart, no questions asked. As the cart rolled down the main road, Eloise was relieved it was full of pears, and not something with a less appealing smell, like durian, pukeweed, or used socks.

The one tricky moment was exiting the castle gates. To almost anyone, she'd look like an ordinary traveller sitting on the back of a cart. But that day, the duty guard was Lorch Lacksneck from Lower Glenth. Eloise was not friends with him, but knew him well enough to say hello. He was a dedicated, respectful wall of muscle and rectitude. Lorch chatted with BB and BdB as he checked them through the castle gate, noting them on the exit scroll. "Say hey to my folks if you see them," he said.

"Will do," BB said.

"And if my mother holds true to form, you'll need the following answers to her questions: Yes, he's eating. Yes, the fungal issue has cleared. No, really, it's cleared up. No, he's not married. Yes, he would tell you beforehand. No, you should not be holding your breath. No, he hasn't forgotten how to write. Yes, he loves you."

As the cart pulled through the gate, Lorch looked up from the exit scroll and caught Eloise's eyes. His brow furrowed, puzzled. He looked down at the scroll and back up at her. She gave him a small wave, then put her index finger across her lips in a "let's keep this quiet" gesture. His furrowed look deepened, and he cocked his head in an unspoken question. Eloise held her thumb and forefinger three weak lengths apart, hoping the narrow gap conveyed a short amount of time. Then she pointed to Jerome, showing that she was not on her own.

Lorch let the cart go, but his face remained neutral and his eyes on her until BdB rounded a corner and the castle gate was no longer in sight.

Eloise's stomach tightened. Would he rush off and tell someone? Would there suddenly be a squadron of guards ready to haul her home? She hoped not. She was really looking forward to a day out. But if a retrieval crew showed up, well, so be it.

They rolled past the town walls and out into the countryside, following the Queen's Roadway for a few strong lengths before turning off onto a smaller road toward Mooondale and Lower Glenth. BB and BdB kept up a steady flow of amiable conversation. It had been BdB's first trip to Brague, and the horse's chatter revealed a gossipy fascination with the castle and town, especially with its equine goings-on. "Did you know, BB, did you know, did you know there are establishments in Brague that are just for horses? Horses only, BB." The horse trotted, neck crooked, keeping one eye on the road while the other looked up at BB in the driver's seat.

"Actually, I had, indeed, heard such things, yes."

"And you didn't tell me beforehand? You left me to figure that out on my own?"

BB wiped a hand across his face. "Never occurred to me to say anything. Sorry. But it's not like you asked, either."

"How am I to know to ask you about something that I don't know exists?"

"Fair point."

"Do you know what goes on in those places?" BdB looked scandalized. "Can you guess?"

"I'm guessing that one might have something to nibble and something to drink. And one might enjoy the company of other horses."

"Yes, yes. Of course, there's that. But gambling, BB! Gambling! They gamble using oats for wagers!"

"BdB, are you telling me that there is gambling taking place right under the nose of our fair queen?"

"Under her nose? No, she wasn't there. Not that I saw."

"Figure of speech, BdB."

"Oh. Sorry, I can't always tell. There was one Percheron there, a huge stallion who wore something that made him smell of flowers."

"Flowers?"

"Flowers, BB. A stallion who smelled of flowers. Like wisteria and frangipani. I smelled it with my own nose. He had a Hanoverian mare on one side and an Arabian mare on the other. He called them his 'good luck charms'. Colt, oh, colt, they were pretty. Anyway, the Percheron was wagering bushels at a time. Bushels, BB! Of oats!"

"Is that a fact, BdB?"

"It is! It is! I saw it with my own eyes, BB."

"Well, that's something. What were they gambling on? Cards? Dice?"

"Humans! They were gambling on humans running foot races! They had this circle, and humans raced around it."

"You don't say, BdB."

"I do say, BB. I say it very much. Humans!"

"Why would anyone wager perfectly good oats on a bunch of humans running in a circle?"

"That is the salient question, BB, I daresay. Made no sense to me at all. No sense at all."

Eloise had never heard of such entertainment in Brague. She caught Jerome's eye and gave a questioning shake of her head. Jerome shook his back. It made her wonder what else went on that she was ignorant of.

"So?" asked BB.

"So what?"

"So, did you place a wager, BdB?"

The horse stopped talking, although the cart kept moving. The pause stretched. Suddenly, Böyden let loose the deepest laugh Eloise had ever heard. "Why, Basilio de Bardigiano, you bet on a human!" His guffaws were infectious, and Eloise found she could hardly keep from laughing herself.

If horses could blush, BdB would have looked like a beetroot.

"Did you... Did you..." BB could barely get the words out through his laughter.

"Did I what?" The horse sounded indignant. He held his chin up and trotted down the road without looking left or right.

"Did you... Did you win?"

Another long pause.

BB howled with laughter, tears trickling from his eyes. "I'm gonna... I'm gonna..."

BdB stopped and turned his neck all the way around, so he was looking straight at his business partner. "Don't."

"I'm gonna, I'm gonna tell your missus!"

"Please, BdB. Please, don't. She wouldn't understand."

"She wouldn't understand? *I* don't understand. You wasted perfectly good oats wagering on humans running around from nowhere to nowhere. Ludicrous! I thought you had more sense than that, BdB."

The horse hung his head, ashamed. "Apparently I don't," he whispered. "I thought it would be fun."

"Was it?" BB's laughter faded.

"No. I felt sorry for the humans, being forced to run around like that. Poor bloody things. I wanted to take them all home with me."

"I'm sure they're fine. Some humans like racing around."

"They didn't look fine, BB. They looked sad. And they didn't look like they had much choice about being there."

That stopped the laughter. It wasn't such a fun or funny idea if someone treated the people badly, or forced them to participate in something exploitative.

The cart rolled down the road for a dozen strong lengths in silence. Eloise thought this might be something she should take up with her mother when she returned.

WAFT! AN AUTUMNAL FESTIVAL

They wound their way through the autumn morning, the cart rolling past a village called Quaint, which it wasn't, and through Working, where there was no sign that anyone did so. Eloise relaxed into the journey, even dozing a little, just long enough to miss an entire tri-village area once settled by mystics and retired scholars—the hamlets of Inner Knowledge, Outer Knowledge, and Cluelessness. The crisp autumn sky was sun-kissed and breeze-caressed, and soft flurries of leaves were visible from half a strong length away. Stands of ash, maple, and silver birch practically screamed at Eloise to enjoy their colors.

"This is beautiful, Jeriffic," Eloise said. "I'm glad you suggested it."

"You haven't seen anything yet. Mooondale makes this look like a hellscape."

"Oh?"

"Yep."

"Well, it must be something, then."

"I look forward to you seeing it. I think you might like it."

Eloise reached over and took his paw. "I'm sure I will."

Around mid-morning they came upon a rough-hewn wooden road sign with an "M" painted on it. Below this, someone had hammered another sign, which read "Waft! An Autumnal Festival". Both signs pointed in the same direction.

"There we go," said BdB. He turned their cart left onto a side road.

It was the grandest avenue Eloise had ever seen. Trees formed a canopy of fall splendor that towered above them, exploding russet and yellow. Of course, Eloise had seen autumn foliage before. There were plenty of deciduous trees in and around the castle grounds. But never anything so majestic or picturesque as this. From the even spacing and repeated pattern of mountain ash, claret ash, and liquidambar, it was clear that someone, decades if not centuries before, had planted this corridor with exactly this result in mind. Eloise sent that unknown person a silent thank you.

Two strong lengths from the turnoff, the road crested a steep rise, then opened out onto a snug valley filled with more color than Eloise had thought possible. From above, it looked like a painter's palette, ready to splash color on a canvas.

"Wow. Just, wow," said Eloise.

"I know, right?" Jerome smiled. "Maybe my mother brought me here a little later in the season. This is even more dazzling than I remember."

BB called to them from the front of the cart. "You folks still OK back there?"

"Yes, thank you," said Eloise. "It's been very pleasant."

"That's good to hear. Is it OK if we drop you at the edge of town? It'll be packed, and hard to drive through."

"And we have pears we need to get home," said BdB.

"Of course, of course," said Jerome.

BdB turned the cart around at the first building they came to, and Eloise and Jerome hopped off.

"You folks take care," said the horse.

"Have a good time," said Böyden.

"I'm sure we will," said Eloise. "Thank you again."

BB gave her a little salute. Moments later, the radish transporters had slipped away into the cover of falling leaves.

Calling Waft! An Autumnal Festival "packed" was an understatement. It was shop-to-shop, inn-to-inn, park bench-to-gazebo full of hundreds of people from dozens of species. A party of goats strolled from tree to tree, nibbling the leaves on the ground below each and commenting on their flavors. A nest of python snakelets slithered around in the leaves, laughing at the rustling sound they made, while their parents flicked out their tongues, tasting the crisp air. In a corner of the public square, a group of children, chimps, and chinchillas piled up leaves then took turns jumping into them. Sweet mongers sold candies in the shape and color of leaves, and face painters decorated faces in a camouflage of autumn colors.

On one street corner, an aging bard busking with a lute croaked out old seasonal standards like "The Falling Leaves of Yore," "Your Falling Leaves," "You're Falling, Leaves," and the always popular "Never Leaf Me Alone". Twenty lengths away, another bard with a wispy beard, a black lute, and a raspy voice busked more modernist autumnal entertainment, including "The Leaves are Falling Like Your Nanna With a Bad Hip", "The Colors of the Season Remind Me of You(r Skin Rash)", and "It's Autumn, and Soon a Lot of You Will Be Dead, or At Least Hibernating".

And the food! Eloise and Jerome wandered through a forest of market stalls offering harvest riches. Yams, gourds, and squash vied for attention with cranberries, brunchberries, and huckleberries. Eloise counted 43 distinct varieties of pumpkin, 22 sorts of beets (including one long-storing variety the farmer called The Beet Goes On), and dozens of apple varieties. And that was just the raw produce. The prepared foods went much, much farther. Eloise got Jerome to buy her a 52-ingredient pumpkin pie, which the stallholder promised would have some pumpkin in it, an acorn alfredo linguini, a slice of deep dish caramel apple pie, a parcel of orange maple sesame balls, a punnet of brunchberries, an apple and cranberry warmer to drink, all followed by an autumn spice haggleberry tea. They shared all of it, except the tea, which Jerome declared a blasphemy against haggleberries everywhere.

Beyond the food, there was plenty of opportunity to take in the beauty of the trees. The people of Mooondale did not dress up in costume, and beyond a few handbills and leaf collages, they let all the attention go to the trees, allowing the autumn colors to speak for themselves. And speak they did, to the glory of all that was natural and great.

They strolled through forest tracks, sometimes with groups of other sightseers, sometimes on their own. Eloise lowered the brunchberry punnet so Jerome could take another. "It's possible that brunchberries are my favorite fruit."

"They wouldn't be a bad choice." Jerome had to eat them carefully— each berry was a third the size of his head, and an errant spray of juice could soak him.

They stopped at a particularly large and colorful cedar. Eloise took a long, deep breath of crisp fall air, and slowly turned in a full circle, taking in the whole area. "This is, without a doubt, one of the most beautiful things I have ever seen. Thank you, Jerome. I'll never forget this."

Jerome smiled. "I'm pleased, Princess Eloise. Really pleased."

They walked back to the village for a last look at the main square. It was coming on mid-afternoon. "It's time we started making our way back to Brague," said Jerome, paying for a hot chocolate. "I'll go arrange something."

"I can come, if you'd like."

"No need. I'll meet you back here."

Eloise settled in to mind their cushion and blankets, and enjoyed some people watching. A lot of people later—more than she would have expected—Jerome returned. From the droop of his whiskers, she could tell the news was not good.

"Nothing," he said.

"Nothing?"

"Zip. Zero."

"No?"

"Carts are still arriving, but none are leaving. Tonight is the festival dance, the Waft! An Autumnal Festival Wingding. Everyone's going. It appears there was a flaw in my planning."

"Could we hire transport? Like a horse or donkey with a cart?"

Jerome shook his head. "I'm sorry, El. I really am. I checked all our options. We can either find a place to spend the night, and hope that it's alright in the morning—that's assuming the inns aren't booked out, which they probably are—or we can hike back up to the turnoff and see if we can catch a lift with passing traffic. If there is any. It's only a couple of strong lengths back."

Eloise pictured her mother, annoyed or angry, perhaps, but definitely more than concerned when she found Eloise absent. And then there was Odmilla. She'd lied to her by omission. If anyone was questioned, it would be Odmilla. Would she try to cover for Eloise, or would she raise an alarm? She'd do whatever she thought was in Eloise's best interests.

Eloise did not like the uncertainty of chancing a ride, but she liked the idea of being a no-show for dinner even less. "Let's try to get home," she said. "It's early enough still. I'm sure we'll find something."

❧ 5 ❧

WOMBANDITOS

They found the road they came in on. To save time, Eloise put Jerome on her shoulder, tucked their cushion and blankets under her arm, and started jogging back through the avenue of trees.

"It's been a while since I've ridden up here," said Jerome. "We used to do this constantly."

"Yes, we were always in a hurry to get to the next thing."

"Not always. We might have hurried to Engineering and Constructions class, or Weapons and Stratagems. I don't remember rushing to Rotes and Recitations, though."

"Or Protocols and Procedures. We were more likely to rush in the other direction."

They made it to the "M" sign before the sun had moved appreciably in the sky, running past carts, horses, donkeys and scores of travelers on foot. The Waft! An Autumnal Festival Wingding would either be a hoot or a riot, given the number of people of all species heading for it. The road toward Brague was empty, but the traffic coming from the Lower Glenth direction was steady.

"Looks promising," said Eloise.

"I hope so. We don't have a lot of wait time built into our schedule."

"True, but we aren't desperate yet."

"No, we're not. Let's stand a little ways up the road, so we don't mistakenly flag down someone going to Mooondale."

They moved to where they had a good view in both directions, set down the cushion and blankets, and prepared to catch the next ride.

Fifteen minutes stretched to 30, and then an hour. Standing ready to hop on a cart or carriage became sitting and waiting patiently, which slid into tossing pebbles and waiting impatiently. The turnoff to Mooondale was exceptionally popular. The road going on to Brague, on the other hand, was as lively as the architectural design for a despot's crypt. The only person going to Brague was a Çalahtist monk, a meerkat on foot who was sworn to silence. Not much help.

Two hours into their wait, Eloise was feeling peckish and antsy (a phrase offensive to ants, she knew). She stood up and said, "I need a private moment."

"Of course. I'll give a yell if someone comes."

"*When* someone comes?"

"Right. When."

Eloise walked 20 lengths into the forest, decided it was still too close to the road, and walked another 30.

There, she found it—the largest stand of brunchberries she'd ever seen. It was half again as tall as she was, untouched, and the berries hung ripe and ready to pick. Normally she'd insist that any fruit was washed carefully before she'd touch it, but they looked so large and ripe that she picked one and popped it straight into her mouth without even wiping it on her sleeve.

Çalaht slurping succotash, it was divine. It was like cherubim came down from on high and sang to her tongue.

She plucked a few more, carefully avoiding the vines' many thorns and ignoring the berry juice staining her hands. She ate a handful all at once. Maybe it was the tiredness of a long day, but Eloise was sure she'd never tasted anything so good in her life. And there were so many. An abundance of brunchberries worthy of a celebration as grand as Waft! An Autumnal Festival. She ran back to where Jerome sat waiting.

"Brunchberries, Jerome! Brunchberries!"

Jerome's eyes went wide. "Really? Where?"

Eloise pointed vaguely in the direction she had come from. "Back there. A ways back." She grabbed the cushion, took it out of its cover, and left the cushion with Jerome. "Won't be a minute." Eloise dashed back to fill the cover with berries. If she didn't eat too many while she was at it, they'd have a cover full of berries for the ride home.

She lost herself in picking, carefully maintaining a 10:1 ratio of berries in the cover to those in her mouth. A quarter hour later, the case was heavy with staining fruit and as full as she could get it without damaging the berries. Eloise sighed, contented, and turned to go back to the road.

That's when she saw them. They had surrounding her. Squint-eyed, hairy nosed, barrel-bodied, and looking tough, unkempt, and ornery.

Wombats. Two dozen ill-clad wombats all pointing swords.

She decided to pretend they weren't threatening her. "G'mid-afternoon to you."

The biggest, squintiest of them moved slowly toward her, sniffing the air. "Well, well, well. What have we here?" He sniffed again. "And she be picking brunchberries for us."

"I'm—"

"Shush! You'll speak when I say you'll speak."

Eloise cradled the cushion cover in her arm and made to walk off—a blustery move given the number of swords between her and the way back. But it was useless. The wombats shifted to block even the slightest opening. With their lousy eyesight, who knew what they might hit if they lunged at her with their blades.

"Who are you?" asked Eloise, defying the order to be silent.

"Wombanditos."

"Wombanditos? Are you a club or something?" asked Eloise.

"We are the Wombanditos! The fiercest gang with bad eyesight in all the realms! Heeyahhhh!" cried the big one.

"Heeyahhhh!" yelled the rest.

"I see. Well, lovely to meet you, but I have to get back to my friend."

"You'll not be going anywhere, Mistress," said the big one. "You'll be coming with us."

"Thank you, but no thank you. I've had a long day, strong lengths to go still, and my friend is waiting for these berries." Without any further discussion, she broke into a run.

Eloise was fast, but the wombats were faster. Three of them tangled her legs and tripped her over. She didn't have time to call out, she just stumbled and fell. Her head struck a rock, and she blacked out.

❧ 6 ❧

IN A BURROW

Eloise awoke in a dark, narrow place. She could barely breathe, and when she tried to move, she realized she was surrounded by dirt.

She was in a burrow. The smells of soil and roots were everywhere.

Her habits screamed. How much grime was getting on her? Was that dirt trickling down the back of her clothes? How much was stuck to her skin?

How on earth had they gotten her in here? Did one of them have a weak magic for cartage?

If she screamed, like her every pore, tissue, and hair wanted to, would anyone hear?

Eloise forced herself to breathe long, slow breaths through her nose. As her pulse eased from dread and fear down to trepidation and agitation, she blinked, waiting for her eyes to adjust. It wasn't completely dark. A streak of green phosphorescence ran along the top, giving shape and shadow to the things in the burrow. No, not things, people. The place was full of wombats, bustling about in the near darkness.

A thousand questions raced through Eloise's head. "How long was I out?" she asked, but it came out, "Hmmma n ha buh uh?" She realized there was a gag in her mouth. She sat up, managing to sit, hunched, in the cramped space. She had barely registered that she was bound with ropes like a felon, when a headache from the fall assaulted her.

A small wombat, obviously set to watch her, startled awake and called out. "Master Shovelhovel! She no be dead. Mumbling be coming out her gob."

The big wombat sidled over to her. "Well, now, RoyLee, that be a good thing. And why?"

"Master Shovelhovel, you always says the live ones is worth more than the deadies."

"And don't you forget that. Now take off her gag so she can speak."

RoyLee did as he was told, and Eloise gulped air that tasted of tilth and loam. She flexed her jaw, relieved at the small freedom. "How long?" she finally asked.

"How long what, Mistress?" asked Shovelhovel.

"How long was I mind-numb?"

"Time, Mistress? Your first question is about time?" Shovelhovel came closer until he was almost touching her. Even in the dim green glow of the burrow, she could tell he was squinting. "We wombats have a very relaxed relationship with time, seeing as we're nocturnal and all, and live in dark burrows."

Now was not the time for her temper. "Could you please do me the kindness of taking your best guess?"

"I can say," chirped RoyLee, eager to be of help.

"Go ahead, young one."

"One dark be gone. The light is just coming up in the east now."

"How can you possibly know that, RoyLee?" asked Shovelhovel.

"My ears be good. I can hear bees. Bees be buzzing at dawn."

Shovelhovel ruffled the tuft of hair on RoyLee's head. "A clever one, you are. I'll not be wasting my time learning what I know to you. Now see if Missus Shovelhovel has any food. Our guest might be hungry soon."

Eloise's mind raced. It was morning! Jerome must be frantic. He must think she'd fallen in a hole, which she more or less had. There was no way she could escape tied up like this. How could she let him know she was alive?

And who knew what chaos her absence had caused at home. She was sure Odmilla would have a very bad day. Were troops being roused? A network of spies activated? Diplomats dispatched? She was Heir and Future Ruler. It's not like she could just slip away.

But that's exactly what she had tried to do.

It had been foolish. And selfish. Other people would be paying the price for a purchase she had made.

Her already low mood sank even further. The conversation she would have with her mother when she got back was not something to look forward to. Not that conversations with her mother ever were.

The best thing she could do was to try to get out of there as fast as she could, and get home as soon as possible, so she could start repairing the damage.

"So your intentions are ransom?" said Eloise.

"Indeed, Mistress," said Shovelhovel.

"And have you made contact with anyone? Have you made any demands?"

"You've no been awake, have you? There's a whole process we go through to ascertain the best methods for doing so."

"I don't like your chances of getting anything," said Eloise.

"That's not what I reckon." Shovelhovel sniffed her again. "You be having the smell of class on you. Just listen to how you be speaking. Feel the quality of the material in your garments. That outfit didna come outta a ragpicker's basket. Plus, the friend you spoke of when we first found you? I think we know who you mean. There's some frantic looking about going on out there."

"You're wasting your time. He has nothing to pay a ransom with."

"We're the Wombanditos. We're patient," said Shovelhovel. "It may not be him we extract your ransom from. He might just be the conduit. Now, would you care for some root soup? My missus makes it special for guests like yourself."

"Thank you, but no thank you," said Eloise. "Not yet. Is there somewhere I might wash up?"

Suddenly, the burrow filled with wombat laughter. "No, Mistress, you'll no be washing up. You're in a wombat burrow, not an inn." Shovelhovel turned and wandered away from her, still chuckling. As the burrow narrowed into a left-hand turn, he called back to her, "Let me know if you change your mind about the soup."

Eloise remained trussed, bored, uncomfortable, anxious, and unable to see anything save wombat shadows for what seemed like a very long, dull time.

7

SOMEONE SHOULD SIT IN A CORNER

Eloise dreamed she heard Jerome. He sounded far away. In a small timorous voice, he politely asked the air, "El? Are you in there?"

Wombats rose at once, drawing swords. "Who goes there?" shouted Shovelhovel, squinting toward the entrance. "Who dares enter the burrow of the Wombanditos, the fiercest gang with bad eyesight in all the realms? Heeyahhhh!"

"Heeyahhhh!" the other wombats screamed in response.

It wasn't a dream. It was Jerome! Thank Çalaht, Jerome had found her. She let out a huge breath and trailed her eyes heavenward. Then she looked toward his voice, trying to locate him. "I'm here!" she called.

"Shush, you!" said RoyLee, and before she knew it, she was wearing the gag again.

Jerome eased himself further into the burrow ignoring the drawn weapons, all polite manners and good grace. "Good evening, ladies and gentlemen. My name is Jerome. I believe you have kidnapped my friend, Eloise."

"Eloise?" asked Shovelhovel. "Like our queen?" He squinted in Eloise's direction. "In violation of the Can't Name Your Child After the Queen edict? Boy, you're lucky she doesn't know you have her name. She'd rip off your arms and legs and swap 'em if she found out."

Eloise shrugged, but couldn't say anything.

"No one in their right mind defies the ban on naming yer sprogs after the queen and king." He turned back to Jerome. "Very brave of you to come in here like that. Now turn around and go out. Any parlaying you want to do will be done outside."

Jerome ignored him. "Did you say your name was the Wombanditos?"

"That we did," said Shovelhovel. "We're the Wombanditos, the fiercest gang with bad eyesight in all the realms! Heeyahhhh!"

"Heeyahhhh!" screamed the others again.

"With all due respect, and I understand how hard it is to come up with good names, that one is terrible. Horrific. Wombanditos? C'mon, really?"

"What? No! It is a fantastic name," insisted Shovelhovel. "It be fierce, like we are. It be setting hearts trembling and knees a'knockin'. Wombanditos! Heeyahhhh!"

"Heeyahhhh!"

Jerome ignored that too. "I mean, I can see what you were going for. You're wombats. You're bandits. So you're looking for a wordplay that captures both. Hence, the portmanteau. I get it."

"That's right!" said Shovelhovel. "We are the Wombanditos, the fiercest gang with bad eyesight in all the realms! Heeyahhhh!"

"Heeyahhhh!" cried everyone yet again.

"I get it, I get it," said Jerome, intentionally looking bored. "But you don't. Whoever let that one get through the approval process needs to go and sit in the corner for a while."

Shovelhovel puffed out his chest, belligerent. "Why say you that?"

"A hundred reasons. No, a thousand reasons. But let's start with one. Look at it when it's written." Jerome scratched out the name with a stick, forming huge letters so they'd legible in the burrow's dim green light, even to squinty-eyed wombats. The wombats lowered their swords and crowded around for a look. "What is at the beginning?"

"W-o-m-b-a," ventured a small voice. It was RoyLee. "That be the start of 'wombats.'"

"But what else is there?" No one said anything. The silence stretched. "Nothing?" asked Jerome. Slowly he covered over the "a" with his foot

"W-o-m-b. 'Wom-b'," said RoyLee, pronouncing the word with a hard "b". "That still be the start of 'wombats'. That no change anything."

"Or it could be..." led Jerome. "Rhymes with 'room'?"

"Womb?" said RoyLee, uncertain.

With that, the room erupted. They had clearly never seen the "womb" lurking in "wombat." But now they had, and they could never un-see it.

"Oh, no!" cried Shovelhovel, his anguish louder than the others. "Womb-banditos! It's like we're stealin' bits from ladies." He clunked his head a few times on the burrow wall. "Not only is that disgustin', but we be bleedin' marsupials! We got no use for wombs. Our women folk has got pouches. What would we be stealin' bits from ladies for?"

There was general agreement in the room.

"I agree. It's a disaster," said Jerome. "The name is a complete carriage wreck. But..."

"But what?" Shovelhovel looked like someone had spat in his soy milk. "We've spent years building up a reputation with that name. Now it be ruined. Ruined! We must be the laughingstock of all the other gangs."

"Yeah, look, sorry about that," said Jerome. "But if there's any way I can get my friend back, we have a naming business we have to get back to. Would it be possible—"

"What?" Shovelhovel grabbed the front of Jerome's tunic and hauled him off the ground. "What did ye say?"

"I said that I was hoping to try to get my friend back from you good people," said Jerome. "She and I run a naming business, and she's the creative genius. I need her if we're going to keep the smart and snappy names coming."

"You have a naming business?" asked RoyLee. "What have you named? Anything famous?"

Jerome looked as embarrassed as he could while dangling by his tunic front. "Oh, I couldn't possibly say. That's all commercial-in-confidence. I mean, I couldn't very well go around saying, 'You know brunchber-ries? They used to be called slugfruit.' A breach of confidentiality like that would be terrible for business. Not that there's anything wrong with slugs, of course."

Shovelhovel shook Jerome a little. "You be telling me that you named brunchberries? They always be named that."

Jerome shook his head slowly and pointed an index claw at Eloise. "She named them. Absolute genius, she is." Shovelhovel looked around at Eloise again, and she gave a self-deprecating nod, indicating that Jerome was right.

Shovelhovel put Jerome down with a small shove. "What else has yer business named?"

Jerome feigned chagrin, like he was divulging naughty secrets. "Have you heard of Lurid Eddie?"

"The carriage maker? Of course," said Shovelhovel.

"He used to be called Bland Bob. Couldn't sell a carriage in a month. But then he had a name change, and boom! Now he can't make them fast enough."

"That be amazing," said RoyLee. "What else?"

"Ever had potato soup?" asked Jerome.

"It be me favorite," said RoyLee.

"Until she got ahold of it, they called it 'bulbous dirt vegetable gruel.'"

"Oh, yuck," said RoyLee, genuinely disgusted. "I'd never eat bulbous dirt vegetable gruel."

"I know, right?" agreed Jerome. "But look, I digress. I really need my creative savant back. So, if you lovely womb-banditos can just—"

"Stop!" yelled Shovelhovel. "Don't be saying our name that way."

"Sorry. I'm not the one who came up with it."

The burrow buzzed with dissatisfaction.

RoyLee raised his paw to speak. "Master Jerome. Do you think you could be doing a new name for us?"

"Well, it is what we do. But you've kidnapped my friend, and I'm really only here to try to talk ransom. How much do you reckon you'll get for her?"

"For the likes of her?" said Shovelhovel. "I reckon 27 coins. Maybe 28."

"Come now, really?" said Jerome in disbelief. "You really think you'll get more than 15 coins for a thin, not-particularly-attractive nobody like her?"

"You just said she was a creative sav—, sav—, a creative genius," said Shovelhovel.

"Well, there is that, I guess," agreed Jerome reluctantly. "But you didn't know that, and the people you're trying to get ransom coin from may not either. A bit iffy, the valuing people thing. Maybe you might get 20 or 21?"

RoyLee tugged Jerome's sleeve again. "How much do a new name cost, Master Jerome?"

"Oh, that depends. We got 95 coins from the Brunchberry Guild, back when they were still the Slugfruit Guild. And if memory serves, we got

123 coins from Bland Bob. So, you know, somewhere in that range. But with overheads and expenses, plus the economic ups and downs..."

"No way!" said RoyLee, impressed. "That be a massive pile of coin."

Jerome gave another nod, and pointed at Eloise again, who also nodded like she was admitting a closely held truth. "Go somewhere like Brague, especially anywhere within a peach pit's throw of the queen and castle, and you'll pay 250 coins for a half-way decent name, and as much as 500 for a really, really good one."

"Amazin'," said RoyLee. "I had no idea names be that expensive."

"We'll swap," said Shovelhovel to Jerome. "Her for a new name."

"Are you out of your womb-bat mind?" Jerome looked offended right down to his stockings. "Our names are worth much, much more than your ransom. That's not a fair deal at all." He turned and started walking toward the burrow entrance. "I won't be insulted like that. Keep her, if that's what you want."

"Stop!" said Shovelhovel.

Jerome did, slowly turning back around. "What? Are you going to insult me again? And in front of my friend. You really should be ashamed of yourself."

"Sorry, matey, sorry," said Shovelhovel. "I meant no offense. But we be needin' a name and you be needin' yer friend, so it seemed, yer know, logical, is all."

Jerome walked back to him. "I guess there might be some logic to it. But you're asking me to lower our price by 60 to 95 coins. That's almost four times the value of your ransom. Four!" He held up four claws for emphasis. "You expect me to accept a deal like that? That is an insult to my mother, Çalaht bless her." He sat on a stone bench, folded his arms, and waited.

"Ten," Shovelhovel finally said.

"Ten what?" Jerome plucked a thread from his pantaloons.

"Ten coins plus the girl," said Shovelhovel. "In exchange for a name. But it gotta be a good one, not just a decent one. If we're going to go through the effort of changing our name, I only wants to do it once."

Jerome sighed like the terms were distasteful. "El?"

Eloise nodded agreement.

Jerome stood and offered his paw to shake. "Deal. Ten coins and my friend's freedom in return for a new name for your fearsome gang."

Shovelhovel shook his paw. "Deal."

❧ 8 ❧

THE NAMING OF WOMBATS

Jerome turned to RoyLee. "Young sir, could you please untie and ungag the creative wonder that is my friend?"

"Leave her bound," commanded Shovelhovel.

Jerome furrowed his brow at the big wombat. "You really don't understand the creative process, do you? For the ideas to flow, she has to have freedom of movement. Free movement fosters free thought. Otherwise, you're going to end up with a name like 'lichen snaggers'— or worse. Untie her. I promise that she will deliver a name you'll be happy with."

Shovelhovel thought for a moment. "RoyLee, untie her—all but her wrists."

"Good enough," said Jerome. RoyLee set to loosening the knots, while Jerome addressed the rest of the wombats. "Now please. We will need to confer. Can you kindly back up and give us space? It will take a little time for the genius to emerge."

Jerome sat down next to Eloise, who was now mostly untied and sitting up. She leaned toward him, grateful he was there. "No sudden moves, El. Just make motions like you're thinking really hard," he whispered. Eloise nodded, and put her bound hands to her forehead, closed her eyes, and started rocking slowly back and forth.

"Thank you for finding me," she whispered. "I had no idea what I was going to do, and the burrow was getting to me."

"Take your time and let the creative waves flow through you," Jerome told her loudly. Then whispering, he added, "Thank goodness you're OK. I've been crashing about the place trying to find you. I was starting to think you were gone for good. Can you moan a bit, for effect?"

Eloise gave a low moan and increased the sway of her rocking. "You were brilliant. And this is ridiculous."

"Think! Think, oh, genius one!" encouraged Jerome for the wombats' benefit, then added quietly, "I don't suppose you have any names for them?"

"What?"

"We have to come up with something. Do you have any names?"

"None that are polite."

"Keep up the moaning. Now sway side to side, just to change it up. Keep going..."

Jerome left Eloise with her hands on her forehead, moaning and swaying from left to right, and walked over to Shovelhovel. "Um, this isn't going as well as I'd hoped."

"Why not?"

"Creativity like hers needs nurturing, encouragement, and proper conditions. When was the last time she ate?"

"She refused our food. And me wife's mighty upset about that, too, matey."

"Fresh air? Has she had the chance to breathe something other than burrow dust?"

"Er, no. We keeps 'em tied up, like you saw. We don't want to be carryin' them in and out all the time."

"Fair enough. It's just..."

"What?"

Jerome sighed. "It's just that I want her to get you the best name she can. She can't do that while she's cooped up like a, um, like a kidnap victim. She needs the inspiration of nature! She needs fresh air in her lungs. Can we get that for her? No, let me say that differently. Can we get that for *you*, since the name will be yours?"

"Oh, alright then. For the name's sake," said Shovelhovel. "Follow me. There's a big opening up the back entrance."

Eloise tried to look lost in a trance as she, Jerome, and the wombats moved out of the burrow. They led her to a clear spot where she and Jerome could sit down.

"Back up, back up," Jerome said to the wombats. "She needs space for her muse to express itself." The wombats still surrounded them, but backed away enough that they could whisper without being overheard. "Got anything?" asked Jerome. "You are, after all, the creative genius of this business."

"Only because you said I was."

"True. OK, make a big show of it for another two minutes. We'll come up with something."

Eloise moaned louder, rocked and swayed, and threw in some wavy arm motions. Jerome let this go on for a dramatically long time, then whispered, "On the count of three stop suddenly, then lean over and pretend to say something to me." Eloise did, reaching a crescendo that involved some drool, a cross-eyed look, and a sudden cessation of all movement. She leaned down to Jerome. "Actually, I've got something." She whispered it in his ear.

Jerome rocked back a little, his eyes widening. "Why, El." He lifted his tail like he was hoisting the purple flag at a hockey sacking match, and mimed chiming the gong. "Two points to the princess."

Jerome stood up and threw his arms wide. "That's brilliant! Perfect!" he exclaimed. "Our clients will be thrilled. You're a genius. You've done it again!"

Eloise bowed to the wombats, sat down, and tried to look her most serene.

Shovelhovel came forward. "So, what she get?"

Jerome held out his paw "Sorry, coins first."

At a nod, RoyLee scampered into the burrow and came back with ten coins in his fist. Jerome took them, bit one, and then dropped them into his pantaloons pocket. He cleared his throat and declaimed, "The Wombanditos are no more! Henceforth, the world shall tremble in fear at the name of the roughest, toughest wombat gang in all the realms—the Pillagiarists."

"The Pill... The Pillagiarists?" Shovelhovel looked unconvinced. "What's it mean?"

"It is your new identity, my friend. Your new brand. It represents all that you are in four simple syllables. The Pillagiarists! It combines 'pillage', which you know."

"Yeah, we like 'pillage'. That's stealin' and stuff."

"And 'plagiarism'."

"Plagiarism?"

Jerome swooped his arm, like he was introducing something grand. "Plagiarism is a form of stealing. So your name has not one, but two— count them, *two* words for stealing in it."

Shovelhovel looked like he was warming to it. "So, from now on, we be the Pill—, the Pillagiarists, the fiercest gang with bad eyesight in all the realms."

"Lose the bit about the eyesight and you have it," said Jerome.

Shovelhovel raised his sword. "We be the Pillagiarists! The fiercest gang in all the realms! Heeyahhhh!"

"Heeyahhhh!" cried the wombats as one.

And with that, Eloise was free.

They said their goodbyes and walked toward the road, and with any luck, a fast ride home.

"Thank you, Jerome," Eloise said as they walked away from the burrow. "Thank you for getting me out of there."

"My pleasure, El. It is what friends are for."

They strolled past the brunchberry stand, but Eloise had lost her desire for them. "Just one thing," she said. "'Thin, not-particularly-attractive nobody.' Really?"

"Just trying to keep the price down, El. Just trying to keep the price down."

✽ 9 ✽
SULKY

It was a relief to be waiting by the road again for the chance to catch a ride, sitting on the blanket and cushion. The cover was gone; it had been commandeered by the Pillagiarists for the brunchberries while Eloise lay mind-numb. By the time she'd woken up, they'd eaten the berries and cut up and sewn the cover into a scarf, a cap, a decorative wall hanging (although no one would ever see it), and a serviette.

"It shouldn't take too long to find someone headed to Brague," said Jerome. "The Waft! An Autumnal Festival wraps up today."

So they waited.

Eloise worked out that it was almost exactly a day since she had found the brunchberry stand, which meant that she would be almost exactly a day late for dinner. It was going to be ugly.

They hadn't been waiting very long when a man with a horse-drawn sulky finally turned in their direction from the Mooondale intersection. The two-seater sulky only had the one person on it. Maybe he'd give them a lift? Jerome could sit on her lap. Eloise and Jerome stood up, ready to wave him down.

As they came up the road, Eloise thought there was something famil-iar-looking about the large, muscly man, and possibly the horse as well —a salt-and-pepper Clydesdale the size of a barn with magnificent white feathering on his feet. Even before Eloise waved, the horse slowed to stop near them. The man was in his early twenties. He wore civilian clothes, so it took her a moment to realize who it was.

"Why, Guard Lorch Lacksneck. What a pleasant surprise."

"Princess Eloise. Master Jerome. Thank Çalaht we found you."

"Found us?"

"Yes, we have been looking for you."

"Oh." Eloise's shoulders drooped. "Looking for a while?"

"A while, yes." Lorch hopped down from the sulky.

"Are you hurt, Princess Eloise? Your clothes..."

Eloise had not been able to brush away all the dirt from her outfit. Clearly, the Pillagiarists had dragged her into their burrow, not carried her. "Yes, I'm fine. It's OK. I fell, but I'm alright." She gently touched the side of her head. "Bit of a bump is all."

"Very good." Lorch gestured toward the horse. "Please allow me to introduce Älbërt de Clydesdale. He's a friend of mine from Lower Glenth, although he's mainly in Brague now."

"Pleased to meet you, Master de Clydesdale. I'm Eloise. This is Jerome Abernatheen de Chipmunk."

Jerome waved hello. He'd instinctively moved to a spot where the horse could see him, so it was less likely he'd get stomped on by a dinner-plate-sized hoof.

"Thank you, Princess Eloise and Master Abernatheen de Chipmunk. Pleased to be making your acquaintances. I'm Älbërt." For such a large horse, he had the voice of a guinea pig.

"Do you mind if we ride in your sulky?" Eloise didn't really need to ask, since it was clear what the purpose was, but it was the polite thing to do.

"My pleasure, Princess Eloise, Master Jerome," Älbërt squeaked. "Hop aboard."

Lorch offered his arm to help her step up. "I don't mean to assume. Are you ready to return to Castle Brague?"

"Yes. Yes, I think I am."

Eloise slid into the seat and lay the blanket across her legs for warmth. Jerome settled on the cushion between her and Lorch.

"Ready when you are, Äl," said the guard.

"Rightio, Lorchio." The horse eased into a walk, then sped up to a trot. At that speed, given how big Älbërt was, they'd be back in Brague in half the time that the radish cart had taken going the other way.

The three travelers rode in silence for several strong lengths. It was an awkward silence. Eloise didn't know Lorch all that well, and after all that had happened, she wasn't sure what she should say to whom. It seemed Lorch was disinclined to chat, and Jerome, who normally filled the air with words, had fallen asleep, head back, mouth agape, issuing small, undignified, chipmunk snores. The effort of finding her must have caught up with him.

Finally, Eloise asked, "Guard Lacksneck, on a scale of, say, 'stern finger wagging' to 'prepare to be flogged and pilloried', just how much trouble am I in?"

"It would be fair to say your absence was noted, Princess Eloise."

"Noted with raised voices? Raised alarms? Raised sticks? Please, Guard Lacksneck. What will I be walking into? Just so I can be ready."

"I spoke only briefly to our queen."

"Right. And what did my mother have to say?"

Lorch's face flushed a little, and he deliberately avoided eye contact. It was as though the topic was uncomfortable for him, and he'd rather not talk about it.

"Guard Lacksneck?"

"It is possible I was not entirely forthcoming with our queen. I'm sorry, Princess Eloise. As such, our queen said, 'Have a nice time, and I shall have words with the princess on your return.'"

"That's it? Words?"

"Words."

"What did you say to her?"

"When I saw you, you indicated that you would not be long. You and Master Abernatheen de Chipmunk were riding with BB and BdB. I guessed where you were going. I mean, who wouldn't want to see Waft! An Autumnal Festival? My family used to go every year when I was growing up. But BB and BdB would not be coming back to Brague for a few days at the soonest. So I guessed you did not have a ride back."

"That is a lot of very good guessing."

"The pieces fit together well enough, Princess." Lorch adjusted his seat so he could look at her more directly. "I stayed on duty at the gate for the rest of the day, and when you had not returned by dusk, I asked Älbërt if he'd be willing to miss his dance class and go on a short trip."

"Dance class?" asked Eloise.

"I do competitive equine gavotte," said the Clydesdale. Without missing a beat, he shifted the clopping of his trot to a graceful set of gavotte moves. Then, just as suddenly, he was back to a straight trot. The sulky barely registered the change.

"Very impressive," said Eloise. She turned back to Loch. "How did you get an audience with my mother?"

"Mistress Odmilla set it up. When I met Her Majesty, I said as little as I could, while conveying that I would be bringing you home after the festival dance."

"Which bought you some time."

"Yes, Princess."

They rode another strong length in silence. Then Eloise said, "Thank you, Guard Lacksneck, for being so observant, and for going beyond what anyone might normally have done."

"It was my pleasure," said Lorch.

"And mine," added Älbërt, throwing in a bit more equine gavotte as punctuation.

❧ 10 ❧

CHEWED

Eloise fully expected to get chewed out by the queen when she got home, and her mother did not disappoint. Eloise went straight to her room, where she had to apologize and explain her absence to Odmilla while the platypus helped her clean up and change. Eloise hoped she could just slip into the dining hall for dinner, so that any rebuke might be tempered by the presence of servants and guests. But that hope disappeared when a herald arrived, summoning her to the Declaiming Room.

Her mother was going with formality. That meant she was somewhere between really, really steamed and absolutely livid.

The thing was, Eloise knew she deserved whatever was coming. So, having tidied herself up and fortified herself with a haggleberry tea, she followed the herald to the Declaiming Room to cop whatever was coming.

The queen sat on the Speaking Throne wearing the Judgment Cape. Eloise had hoped for the Attention Cape at least, or maybe the Adjudication Cape. Nope.

The herald stood at the doorway and announced, "Princess Eloise to see the queen."

Queen Eloise had a pile of scrolls stacked on the table next to her, and one lay unfurled on her lap desk, which she was writing on. Eloise entered the room, curtsied, then bent to one knee, lowered her gaze to the floor, and waited.

The queen did not even glance her way. The quill scratching seemed to go on forever. Eventually, without pausing her writing, the queen said, "How many?"

"How many?" repeated Eloise, confused. "I'm sorry, how many what?"

"How many people?" The queen dipped her quill and continued whatever it was she was doing.

Eloise kept her head down, but glanced up slightly, trying to work out what her mother was writing. A list, perhaps? "Apologies, my queen. I do not have the context or reference point for your question."

"The context is clear enough. Your..." She wrote some more. "The context is your absence. As for a reference point..." More writing. "The reference point is those affected. How many people do you reckon you worried, inconvenienced, or brought under suspicion by failing to declare your intentions before engaging in an allegedly spontaneous outing?"

Eloise swallowed. She didn't particularly like where this was going. "I don't know. I've not thought about it."

"Obviously not." The queen finished the second column of whatever she was doing and started writing a third. "Take a guess. Feel free to round down."

Eloise had no idea where this was going. "A dozen, perhaps. Maybe twenty?"

That stopped the queen, who looked straight at her. "Twenty? Twenty?" She gestured at the scroll. "I'm already up to 92. I'm guessing I'm only two-thirds of the way there."

"My queen, I'd like to apologize for my behavior. It was unthinking and irresponsible."

"Keep going."

"Self-centered, impulsive, and inconsiderate."

"And?"

"Keep going?"

"Yes, keep going."

"Is there something in particular?"

"You might say something about putting yourself in harm's way. Or causing distress to your family and those charged with your care and protection. You could add that you were gullible, if you believed you could just sneak off without consequences, intended or unintended. I'm sure the radish monger told you a fine tale about the glories of that Waft! An Autumnal Festival. I hear it is pretty."

"No, ma'am. He didn't—"

"You're lucky that Guard Lacksneck was intending to go to the festival dance on his time off with his friend the dance instructor. Apparently his family goes every year. He volunteered to keep an eye on you and little Jerome, and provide you a ride home that did not involve sitting next to fresh produce." The queen continued writing. "I assented. It was easier and less obtrusive than sending a squadron of guards to find you. I trust you had a good time? Did you have the punch? I hear the punch is nice. All those autumn ingredients. Did you dance?"

"Again, my queen, I'm sorry."

"Well, that makes everything OK, doesn't it?"

Her mother wasn't sarcastic often. That made this chat even more disconcerting. Eloise calmed herself by counting the pieces of wood in the parquetry floor.

The queen let a silence settle while she continued writing. Eloise remained on one knee, head still down. That she had not been allowed to stand was another sign of how badly peeved her mother was.

After a few more dips of the quill, the queen put the feather down and blew on the ink to dry her writing. "There. I've made it an even 120. That's only 100 more than you guessed." The queen handed the scroll to Eloise. "Have a look. Tell me if you think I have listed anyone who should not be there."

Eloise scanned the list. The first few names were obvious. Her parents. Lorch. "Guard Lorch Lacksneck's friend—the one who dances." Jerome's mother, Seer Maybelle de Chipmunk. Odmilla. Eloise's sister Johanna (in the category of inconvenienced, presumably, not worried or under suspicion). Those were all fair enough. Then came less obvious names. "Chef? The Venerable Prelate Herself? And who is Baron Baggerlader von Ellbogen?"

"Chef, because she was inconvenienced in preparing meals that you were not around to eat. The Venerable Prelate Herself, as I had to ask if you'd shown up in any of her devotional houses, not that you would, but it seemed worth checking. Baron Ellbogen is a minor noble from the southwest of The South, who made the journey here to try to interest me in importing more of the cannellini beans grown in his region. He had to be put off for a day, since attention had to be diverted to ascertaining if you'd been apprehended or endangered."

"I left a note."

"A note that lied by omission. Something that was obvious from the most cursory of readings. If you plan to dissemble in the future, I suggest you do a better job of it than that."

Eloise said nothing.

"What do you intend to do about this situation?"

"I've returned. I'm safe. I appreciate that others have been affected, more than I'd anticipated, and am I contrite. I will not do it again, so lesson learned. Is that not enough?"

Queen Eloise leaned back in her chair and adjusted the Judgment Cape across her lap. "No. Not enough." She drummed her fingers on the arm of the Speaking Throne. "Stand."

Eloise got to her feet, laced her hands in front of her, looked her mother in the eye, and waited.

"Eloise, our decisions have consequences. As heir and future ruler, this applies to you more than most. I suggest you should come to terms with some of your consequences."

"Yes, my queen."

"Here is what you will do. You will find each of the people on this list. You will go to them, apologize for having committed a transgression that directly affected them, and then you will ask them for their forgiveness. They'll either give it to you or they won't. That's of little import. You'll then offer to do something for them to try to make amends, or at least balance the scale somewhat."

Eloise's face reddened, and she swallowed. She had to embarrass herself 120 times? "Amends? Like what?" How could she make amends with 120 different people?

"That will be up to you and the person. But it has to be meaningful, or it doesn't count. I expect you to present a record of what, who, and when. Have it done by the end of the month."

"By the end of the month? That's, that's..."

Queen Eloise raised a hand, cutting off any protest. "Is the task clear?"

"Yes, my queen."

"Then I suggest you start with your handmaid, Odmilla. She did not have a good day yesterday. Then go find Baron von Ellbogen so you don't have to make a trip to The South."

"Yes, my queen."

"Do you have anything to say?"

"No, my queen."

"Then you may go and get started."

"Yes, my queen. Thank you for helping me understand the error of my ways."

"No need to be snarky. Now go."

Eloise curtsied and headed for the Declaiming Room door. Just as she reached it, her mother said, "One other thing."

Eloise reluctantly turned to face her, wondering what other embarrassments her mother would foist on her. "Yes, my queen?"

"Did you and Jerome really get ten coins in return for your freedom and a name for that wombat gang?"

Eloise's jaw dropped. How could her mother possibly know about that? And so soon. Her network of informants must truly be incredible. Or maybe she'd already spoken to Jerome. "Yes, my queen. We did."

And for the first time since Eloise entered the room, her mother smiled. "Clever. Well done, the two of you. There's a place for clever, especially for one who will one day sit on this seat, although I hope that day will not be too soon. Now, go. I will see you at dinner."

"Yes, my queen."

"I think 'mother' will do."

"Yes, Mother. Thank you."

EPILOGUE: POT-SCRUBBER

Eloise was elbow-deep in sudsy hot water, scrubbing a crust of cannellini bean soup from the bottom of a huge, feast-day-sized pot—one of a dozen stacked around her—using a mixture of sand, soap, and brute force. She hadn't done this kind of manual work for Chef in two years, not since before her Thorning Ceremony. There was a comfort to being back in the kitchens wearing a servant's outfit. Even though she was officially making her amends for transgressing against Chef, she didn't mind it so much. Plus, it was a warm task to undertake on a brisk autumn day.

Jerome sat on the shelf above the basin nibbling an almond a third of the size of his head and keeping her company.

Eloise paused, marveling at just how stubborn cannellini remnants could be. "You know what I heard yesterday?"

"Nope."

"There was a bard practicing in the Music Hall during the afternoon. Turns out, he was composing a new ditty about a gang of wombats. Our name for them made an appearance. Uncredited, of course."

"Serious? It's only been a couple of weeks."

"Apparently they're the fiercest gang with bad eyesight in all the realms, and the bard wanted to capture their glory in song."

"They didn't drop the bit about the eyesight?"

"Apparently not."

"Well, good luck to them." Jerome took another bite of his almond, then gestured toward the pots. "Do you regret going?"

"I regret how I went, but I don't regret going. It was fun—at least the bits that didn't involve getting dragged underground."

"No, that was not a highlight."

"But in one sense, it was."

"Oh, how so?"

Eloise bore down with a handful of sand, attacking the intractable burned bean crust, finally convincing it to let go of the pot.

"El?"

"I don't know. It was scary, but I got to see a part of the world I'd never seen before, even if it was underground and hard to see. Plus, I got to experience you doing something you're good at—talking off the top of your head."

"Always an honor."

"Sure, for some value of 'honor'. And if I hadn't been kidnapped by the wombats, I wouldn't have had to make amends, which means I wouldn't have engaged with all the people on that list. I've learned heaps of stuff. Did you know that Baron Baggerlader von Ellbogen's favorite bean is actually black beans, but that they don't grow in his part of The South?"

"Fascinating."

"It is, though. I've learned all kinds of interesting things like that."

Eloise worked in silence for a while. The only noise was the scratching of sand on metal and the splashing of water.

Jerome raised a claw and pointed. "You missed a spot, Princess Eloise."

Eloise paused and looked at him. "Really? You're going to do that?"

Very slowly, Jerome raised his tail, a mock hockey sacking scorekeeper. "Point to the pot," he said, then ducked behind one of the pots, giggling, to avoid being soaked by a wave of cannellini water.

Thank you for reading *The Wombanditos*!

This book is a prequel to *The Purple Haze*, book one in the Western Lands and All That Really Matters series. The Purple Haze starts about six months after this book finishes, and tells the story of Princess Eloise as she sets out on a quest to find her kidnapped sister and bring her back home. Jerome is there with her every step of the way, as is Lorch Lacksneck. It's a rollicking quest full of weak magic, stupidly long names, animals who talk, and wäÿ töö mänÿ ümläüts.

Also, if you haven't done so yet, you should sign up for my newsletter to stay on top of new releases and all the latest.

THANK YOU

Thank you for reading The Wombanditos. Reviews are crucial for helping other readers discover new books to enjoy. If you want to share your love for Eloise and Jerome, please leaving a review. I'd really appreciate it.

Recommending my work to others is also a huge help. Feel free to give this book and the whole series a shout-out in your favourite book recommendation group to spread the word.

NEXT IN SERIES

AVAILABLE NOW

Her twin abducted. A treacherous rescue mission. Can an unproven princess escape a prophecy of doom?

If you like tongue-in-cheek humor, vivid medieval worlds, and clever cultural references, then you'll love the first book in this lively adventure. *Read The Purple Haze today* (and get it using the QR code below).

NEXT IN SERIES

ACKNOWLEDGMENTS

It is a joy to get to say thank you to those who have helped me bring this book to the world.

Tamsin Dean Einspruch, our daughter, has from the word go been my first port of call for ideas, perspective, and thoughts on words. She is my first reader, and has been with this story every step of the way. In fact, it was her idea to let the Wombanditos be the core of their own side story, once they were edited out of where they first appeared, which was late in *The Purple Haze*, book one of the Western Lands and All That Really Matters series. I'm glad they did not stay on the cutting room floor.

Many, many thanks to Cheryl Hannah, Janet Watson Kruse, and Olivia Martinez for their beta reads. Cheryl, Janet and Olivia all brought keen eyes to the words, and provided very different perspectives to what they read. Valuable and valued input all.

Thank you to my editor, Vanessa Lanaway, and my proofreader Abigail Nathan. Sharp eyes and red pens, both. Y'all rock. It's that simple.

Thank you to Maria Spada for the fantastic cover.

A huge, massive thank you to my bride, Billie Dean, who reads and gives incredible input on everything I write, who has encouraged me forever, and who believed in my creative soul much, much earlier than I ever did. I love you and I thank you. L^3.

And finally, thank you to you, whoever you are, for picking up this book and having a read. I appreciate it very much.

Andrew Einspruch

June 2018

ABOUT THE AUTHOR

Andrew Einspruch is fond of the wordy, the nerdy, and the funny, which means that if you arranged for him to have lunch with Weird Al Yankovic, Tom Lehrer, William Gibson, and any of the Monty Python guys, he'd be your friend forever. Visit his web site for a complete list of his books at andreweinspruch.com

Andrew is an ex-pat Texan living in Australia, and is the co-founder of the not-for-profit charity the Deep Peace Trust, which fosters deep peace and non-violence for all species. With his wife and daughter, he runs the Trust's farm animal and wild horse sanctuary. (You can see why there's the odd animal or two in his books.)

If pressed, he'll deny he ever coded in COBOL for a bank.

If you haven't done so yet, use the QR code below to jump into the full adventure of The Western Lands and All That Really Matters series.